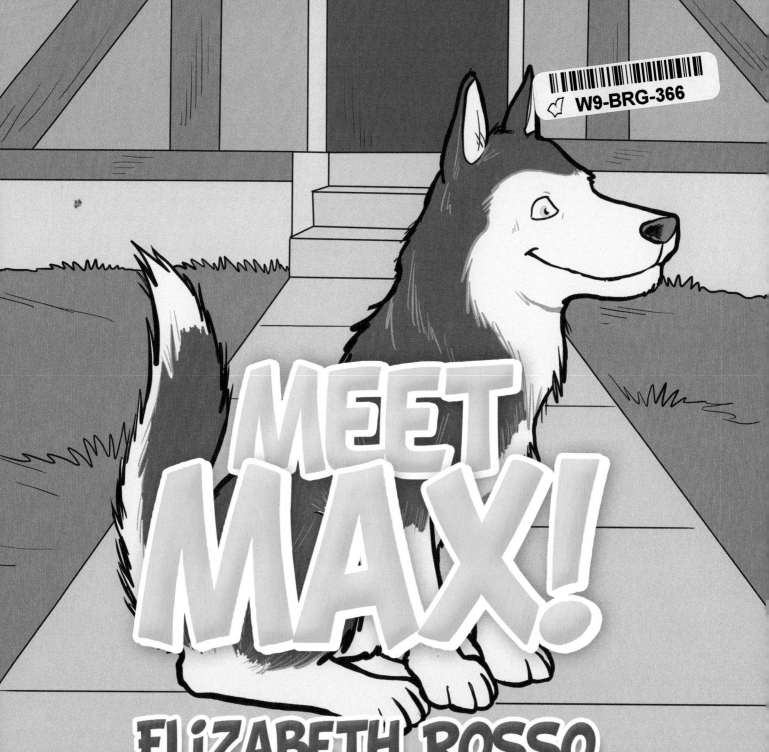

MEET MAX!

ELIZABETH ROSSO

Archway Publishing books may be ordered through booksellers or by contacting:

Archway Publishing
1663 Liberty Drive
Bloomington, IN 47403
www.archwaypublishing.com
1 (888) 242-5904

Because of the dynamic nature of the Internet, any web addresses or links contained in this book may have changed since publication and may no longer be valid. The views expressed in this work are solely those of the author and do not necessarily reflect the views of the publisher, and the publisher hereby disclaims any responsibility for them.

Any people depicted in stock imagery provided by Thinkstock are models, and such images are being used for illustrative purposes only.
Certain stock imagery © Thinkstock.

ISBN: 978-1-4808-2630-4 (sc)
ISBN: 978-1-4808-2629-8 (e)

Print information available on the last page.

Archway Publishing rev. date: 12/31/2015

FOR YUKON,

WHO TOOK ME ON MY FIRST ADVENTURE

THIS IS MAX. MAX IS A VERY BIG DOG.
HE HAS A VERY BUSHY TAIL!

OF COURSE, MAX WAS NOT ALWAYS SO BiG.
HE WAS A VERY SMALL PUPPY.

HE WAS SMALLER THAN ALL OF HiS
BROTHERS AND SiSTERS!

ONE DAY, A LADY CAME TO VISIT.
SHE PLAYED WITH MAX AND SCRATCHED HIS EARS.

MAX LOVED HER!

THEY ALL LIVED IN A HOUSE NEAR A LAKE.

"I LOVE YOU, MAX," THE LADY SAID.
"HOW WOULD YOU LIKE TO COME LIVE WITH ME?"

"OH, BOY!" THOUGHT MAX.
"WHAT AN ADVENTURE THAT WOULD BE!"

THEY GOT iNTO THE CAR.
MAX LOVES CAR RiDES!

HE CRAWLED INTO THE LADY'S LAP.
IT WAS SOFT AND WARM.

THE LADY PETTED MAX GENTLY.
HE LOOKED OUT THE WINDOW AS THEY DROVE.

"DO YOU SEE ALL THE TREES AND HOUSES, MAX?" THE LADY ASKED.

"YES!" THOUGHT MAX.

"WE ARE ALMOST HOME," THE LADY SAID.
"THEN WE WILL HAVE LOTS OF ADVENTURES!"

MAX WAGGED HIS BUSHY TAIL AND
THOUGHT, "I CAN'T WAIT!"

WHAT SORT OF ADVENTURE DiD YOU HAVE TODAY?

CPSIA information can be obtained
at www.ICGtesting.com
Printed in the USA
LVOW01s0615280116
472578LV00002B/2/P